Dear Parents:

Congratulations! Your child is taking the first steps on an exciting journey. The destination? Independent reading!

STEP INTO READING® will help your child get there. The program offers five steps to reading success. Each step includes fun stories and colorful art or photographs. In addition to original fiction and books with favorite characters, there are Step into Reading Non-Fiction Readers, Phonics Readers and Boxed Sets, Sticker Readers, and Comic Readers—a complete literacy program with something to interest every child.

Learning to Read, Step by Step!

Ready to Read   Preschool–Kindergarten
• big type and easy words • rhyme and rhythm • picture clues
For children who know the alphabet and are eager to begin reading.

Reading with Help   Preschool–Grade 1
• basic vocabulary • short sentences • simple stories
For children who recognize familiar words and sound out new words with help.

Reading on Your Own   Grades 1–3
• engaging characters • easy-to-follow plots • popular topics
For children who are ready to read on their own.

Reading Paragraphs   Grades 2–3
• challenging vocabulary • short paragraphs • exciting stories
For newly independent readers who read simple sentences with confidence.

Ready for Chapters   Grades 2–4
• chapters • longer paragraphs • full-color art
For children who want to take the plunge into chapter books but still like colorful pictures.

STEP INTO READING® is designed to give every child a successful reading experience. The grade levels are only guides; children will progress through the steps at their own speed, developing confidence in their reading. The F&P Text Level on the back cover serves as another tool to help you choose the right book for your child.

Remember, a lifetime love of reading starts with a single step!

Visit us on the Web!
StepIntoReading.com
rhcbooks.com

Educators and librarians, for a variety of teaching tools, visit us at
RHTeachersLibrarians.com

Library of Congress Cataloging-in-Publication Data is available upon request
ISBN 978-0-593-43224-2 (trade) — ISBN 978-0-593-43225-9 (lib. bdg.)

Printed in the United States of America
10 9 8 7 6 5 4 3 2 1

This book has been officially leveled by using the F&P Text Level Gradient™ Leveling System.

Random House Children's Books supports the First Amendment and celebrates the right to read.

STEP 3
STEP READING ON YOUR OWN

STEP INTO READING®

CORDUROY'S
Garden

by Allison Inches
illustrated by Allan Eitzen
based on the characters created by Don Freeman

Random House 🏠 New York

Dig! Dig! Dig!

Plop! Plop! Plop!

Pat! Pat! Pat!

"There!" said Lisa.

"My beans are all planted."

Lisa watered the seeds.

Then she picked up Corduroy.

"Come on, Corduroy," she said.

"I have an important job for you."

She took Corduroy inside and
put him in a chair by the window.
"I want you to watch the beans,"
said Lisa.
Then off she went to school.
"Wow," said Corduroy.
"I get to watch the beans!"

Corduroy got right to work.

He watched and watched.

He saw a man next door raking

and a lady walking her baby.

Soon, the sun began to

feel warm.

Corduroy yawned.

Ha hum!

Then Corduroy fell sound

asleep.

Jingle! Jingle! Jingle!

A puppy pushed open the gate

and began digging.

Dirt hit the window.

Corduroy woke up

and looked out.

"Oh no!" cried Corduroy.

"The beans!"

Rap! Rap! Rap!

Corduroy rapped on the window.

But the puppy kept digging.

And digging.

Then *plunk!*

The puppy put his bone

in the hole.

Flick! Flick! Flick!

He buried it

and left the garden.

"I have to find more seeds!"

said Corduroy.

Corduroy looked in Lisa's desk.

He looked under the bed.

"Why, here are some seeds!"

said Corduroy.

Corduroy put three seeds in his
pocket and went to the garden.

Dig! Dig! Dig!

Plop! Plop! Plop!

Pat! Pat! Pat!

"There!" said Corduroy.

"The beans are

all planted again."

"This time," said Corduroy,

"I will make sure

to watch the beans."

And he did.

He watched them on sunny days.

He watched them on rainy days.

He watched them on all the days

in between.

Soon three little shoots came up.

They grew and grew.

The stems wrapped around

the stakes.

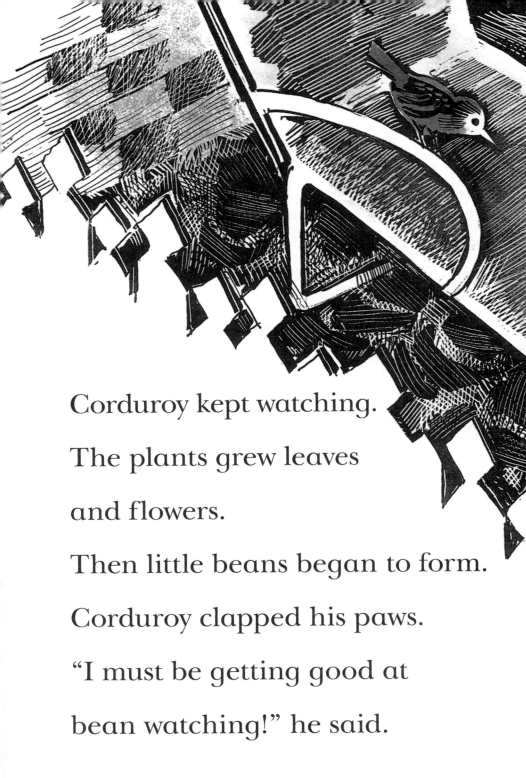

Corduroy kept watching.

The plants grew leaves

and flowers.

Then little beans began to form.

Corduroy clapped his paws.

"I must be getting good at

bean watching!" he said.

He put on his sunglasses
and got back to work.

Then *Jingle! Jingle! Jingle!*

Oh no! thought Corduroy.

The PUPPY!

The puppy was back for his bone.

The puppy stopped

and looked at Corduroy.

His ears went up.

"Arf!" said the puppy.

Corduroy shut his eyes.

But the puppy did not

take the bone.

He took Corduroy instead!

The puppy played toss

with Corduroy.

Corduroy flew up and down,

up and down!

Then the man next door said,

"NO!"

Thunk!

Corduroy fell to the ground.

The man picked Corduroy up
and dusted him off.
"I know where you live,"
said the man.
He took Corduroy home.
And just in time.

The school bus stopped out front.

Lisa ran through the garden gate.

"Oh, look!" she cried.

"I see beans on the vine!"

She picked up Corduroy

and ran to see.

Lisa held a bean in her hand.

She turned it from side to side.

"Oooh," said Lisa.

"This is *not* a bean!"

It's not? thought Corduroy.

Then what is it?

"It's a green pepper!" said Lisa.

A green pepper, thought Corduroy.

Is that good?

"I *love* green peppers!" said Lisa.

Oh, phew! thought Corduroy.

"Corduroy, you did a great job."

I always wanted to do a great job,

thought Corduroy.